CHICAGOLAND
DETECTIVE AGENCY
Nº 1

The Drained Brains Caper

TRINA ROBBINS
ILLUSTRATED BY TYLER PAGE

GRAPHIC UNIVERSE™ · MINNEAPOLIS · NEW YORK

STORY BY **TRINA ROBBINS**

PENCILS AND INKS BY **TYLER PAGE**

LETTERING BY **ZACK GIALLONGO**

Copyright © 2010 by Lerner Publishing Group, Inc.

Graphic Universe™ is a trademark of Lerner Publishing Group, Inc.

Graphic Universe™
A division of Lerner Publishing Group, Inc.
241 First Avenue North
Minneapolis, MN 55401 U.S.A.

Website address: www.lernerbooks.com

Library of Congress Cataloging-in-Publication Data

Robbins, Trina.
     The drained brains caper / by Trina Robbins ; illustrated by Tyler Page.
        p.   cm. — (Chicagoland detective agency ; #01)
     Summary: Required to attend summer school after moving to Chicagoland, thirteen-year-old manga-lover Megan Yamamura needs help from twelve-year-old computer genius Raf Hernandez to escape the maniacal principal's mind-control experiment.
     ISBN: 978-0-7613-4601-2 (lib. bdg. : alk. paper)
     1. Graphic novels. [1. Graphic novels. 2. Conformity—Fiction. 3. Schools—Fiction. 4. Computer programs—Fiction. 5. Japanese Americans—Fiction. 6. Latin Americans—Fiction. 7. Science fiction.] I. Page, Tyler, 1976– ill. II. Title.
PZ7.7.R632Aae 2010
[Fic]—dc22   2009032620

Manufactured in the United States of America
1 – BC – 7/15/10

I'M *NEW* IN TOWN. MY DAD GOT A BETTER JOB, SO WE MOVED HERE TO *CHICAGOLAND*.

IT'S A GOOD THING TOO...

...'CAUSE I WAS KINDA POLITELY ASKED TO *LEAVE* MY OLD SCHOOL.

Grunt

SO, RAF, DO YOU LIKE *POETRY*?

IT JUST SO HAPPENS THAT I'M A POET.

Grunt

I WRITE *HAIKU*.

DO YOU KNOW WHAT *HAIKU* IS?

IT'S A KIND OF *JAPANESE POETRY* THAT CONSISTS OF THREE LINES OF FIVE, SEVEN, AND FIVE SYLLABLES.

Grunt

LIKE:
WHAT ARE YOU MISSING
HIDING BEHIND YOUR SMALL SCREEN?
THERE'S A WORLD OUT THERE.

SO, UM, WHAT'S THAT?

IT'S A NEW *PROGRAM* I'M INVENTING, AND IT'S *WAY MORE* THAN JUST A PROGRAM.

I CALL IT *DELETE*, AS IN...

AMSCRAY, GO AWAY, AND DON'T LET THE DOOR HIT YOU ON THE WAY OUT!!!

OKAY, I CAN TAKE A HINT.

JEEZ! TARANTULAS!

WE DO NOT SELL AN

7

Another morning!
Dad hides behind newspaper
I've got my manga.
—by Megan Yamamura, age 13

DAD, I COULDN'T GET A TARANTULA YESTERDAY. BUT I'LL KEEP LOOKING!

MMM-HMMM

BY THE WAY, PUMPKIN,

YOU'LL HAVE TO SPEND THIS SUMMER IN *SCHOOL.*

BUT, DAD!

I'VE ENROLLED YOU IN A *VERY EXPENSIVE* PRIVATE SUMMER SCHOOL, STEPFORD PREPARATORY ACADEMY, SO YOU CAN CATCH UP AND ENTER YOUR NEW SCHOOL IN NINTH GRADE THIS SEPTEMBER.

BUT, *DAD!*

YOU *MISSED* A LOT OF SCHOOL WHEN YOU HAD TO *LEAVE* AFTER SETTING THE BUILDING ON FIRE.

DAD, I DIDN'T SET FIRE TO THE SCHOOL!

YOU SET OFF THE SPRINKLER SYSTEM, PUMPKIN.

AND THE FIRE ALARM.

CHEF'S SURPRISE. COME AND GET IT.

TODAY'S hot Menu Chefs Surprise

YUCK, NO WAY. I'M A *VEGETARIAN.*

NOW, NOW, MISSY.

Yogurt

MUST EAT YOUR YUMMY *SLOPPY JOE.* WE HERE AT STEPFORD PREP WANT OUR STUDENTS TO GROW UP TO BE HEALTHY YOUNG CITIZENS.

IF ONE TRAIN DEPARTS THE STATION, TRAVELING AT *30 MILES PER HOUR*...

SOOOO BORED... FALLING ASLEE...

WOOP!

TOM HAS *FIVE APPLES*! TRAIN LEAVES STATION AT 30 MILES PER HOUR! *WOOP!* HOW MANY APPLES DOES MARY HAVE? *WOOP!*

HUH?

OH, DEAR.

HOW LONG DID THE TRIP THERE TAKE IF THE RETURN TRIP TOOK *SIX HOURS*? *WOOP!*

HEH. NOTHING SERIOUS, HE'LL BE *RIGHT AS RAIN* IN NO TIME.

WOOP! WOOP! JANE MIXED TOGETHER *FIVE GALLONS* OF ORANGE JUICE AND THREE GALLONS OF APPLE JUICE. *WOOP!* WHAT WAS THE TRAIN'S *AVERAGE SPEED?*

NOW LET'S TURN TO PAGE 25 IN OUR BOOKS...

?

WOOP! IT TAKES JAMES *SEVEN HOURS* TO CLEAN AN ATTIC, BUT MARY CAN CLEAN THE SAME ATTIC IN *FIVE HOURS*. WOOP! WOOP!

THERE WAS THIS REALLY CUTE BOY IN MY CLASS, BUT HE DIDN'T KNOW I WAS ALIVE.

SO I WROTE HIM A *NOTE*...

WELL, A *HAIKU*, REALLY.

Here I sit alone
There's you—baseball
cap backwards
Couldn't we hang
out?

BUT HE PROVED UNWORTHY OF MY AFFECTIONS.

SO I **STOLE** MY HAIKU BACK.

...BUT WHEN I **BURNED** THE HAIKU IN THE SINK IN THE GIRL'S ROOM, IT SET OFF THE SPRINKLERS.

HAHA HAHA!

SO I TOTALLY GOT **EXPELLED** FROM SCHOOL.

HAH... HEH... WHOO! MEGAN, THAT'S **AWESOME!**

DOES THAT MEAN WE'RE FRIENDS?

SO CAN I HAVE YOUR **CELL PHONE NUMBER?** AND YOUR **E-MAIL ADDRESS?**

CHAPTER THREE:
MEGAN HAS HER HEAD EXAMINED

WAKEY, WAKEY!

HOPE YOU'RE COMFY!

CHAPTER FOUR:
THE BRAIN OF A MANIAC!

Mmmrf!

Take the elevator to the roof. We'll be safe there for a while.

RAF, *COME ON!*

NO...

B-BUT WHERE ARE *YOU* GOING?

THEY'RE LOOKING FOR *YOU*, NOT *ME*. I SHOULD BE ABLE TO GET *PAST* THEM.

I'LL BE BACK AS FAST AS I CAN.

TRUST ME.

COWARD! YOU'RE *DESERTING* US!

PUFF PUFF

OH *NOOOOO!*

WILLIAM!

BUT, MOM...

NO *BUTS*, WILLIAM. THAT DOG HAS TO GO.

I'M HOLDING DOWN *TWO* JOBS, AND I *STILL* CAN'T MAKE ENDS MEET. FOOD GETS MORE *EXPENSIVE* EVERY DAY.

AND THAT *DOG* OF YOURS EATS LIKE AN ELEPHANT. I SIMPLY CAN'T FEED US AND FEED HIM TOO.

YOU'LL JUST HAVE TO TAKE HIM BACK TO THE *SHELTER.*

AW, MOM...

LET'S GO TO THE MALL!

I WANNA PLAY SOCCER!

HEY, WHO WAS THAT WACKO ON THE SKATEBOARD?

I THINK YOU'LL FIND THAT STEPFORD HAS BECOME A *HARMLESS PREP SCHOOL*, NOW THAT DR. VORSCHAK'S N.U.T.S. NEVER EXISTED.

RAF, SOMETHING *WEIRD* IS HAPPENING TO YOUR FILE.

OH NOOOOO! MY DELETE PROGRAM IS DELETING *ITSELF!*

MUST'VE BEEN A *GLITCH* IN MY PROGRAMMING!

GOTTA TRY TO-- IT'S NOT WORKING-- I'M *LOSING* IT...

TIP TIP TIP

GAAHH!

SORRY!

Login: **chicagoland**

Password: •••••••n|

Click here to interFACE

MYBLOGFACE

CHICAGOLAND
DETECTIVE AGENCY

InforFACEtion

Location: Behind the counter of Hernandez & Sons Pet Supplies

Hours: 9–5 during summer vacation. During the rest of the year, afterschool hours, except on weekends

Proprietor: Raf Hernandez (that's me) because it's my mom's store

Our motto:
Sad? Scared? Need help fast?
Chicagoland Detectives:
We can do the job!

The Chicagoland Detective Agency is here for you. We solve low crimes and misdemeanors, and we battle injustice. Don't be afraid to come in with your pets. We love animals.

 William Hey, dude, thanks for helping me keep my dog. The Chicagoland Detective Agency rules!

July 18 at 1:15 PM

Friendly FACErs

3 Friends

 Bradley

 Megan Yamamura

 William Johnson

Raf Hernandez's Bio ✉

Favorite quote:
Wherever you are, there you are.

About Me:
When I was five years old, my mom discovered that I was writing math problems on her computer, so she bought me one of my own. I guess that makes me a computer geek. But it also makes me qualified to solve crimes the twenty-first century way: by using computer technology while my assistant, Megan Yamamura, does the legwork.

Ice cream: Chocolate or vanilla?
Rocky road.

Food: Hamburger or fried chicken?
Fried chicken, but my mom won't let me have it unless it's free-range. That means that instead of being stuck in tiny, cramped boxes where they can't even move, the chickens get to run around and peck at stuff on the ground.

Meet the FACE

Raf Hernandez
Age: 12
Education: James A. Garfield Middle School

MYBLOGFACE

Meet the FACE

Megan Yamamura
Age: 13
Education: Stepford
Preparatory Academy

Profession: Detective

Friendly FACErs

3 Friends

Bradley

Raf
Hernandez

William
Johnson

Megan Yamamura's Bio   ☒

Favorite quote:
An old pond
A frog jumping in—
The water's splash
(How cool is that? It's the most famous haiku in the world,
by the great Japanese poet, Basho.)

About Me:
I'm a poet, and my fave poetry is haiku, so that's what I write. Haiku is a form of Japanese poetry in three lines. In Japanese (even though not always in translation—see above!), the first and last lines have five syllables and the middle line has seven syllables, so that's how I write mine. You're probably thinking, pretty easy, I can do that. But actually haiku is supposed to paint a picture with words, to create a mood or feeling in just seventeen syllables, and that's not as easy as you think. Like that poem about the frog: can't you imagine sitting by that pond, and it's really quiet, and then—plop!

The haiku I write are not quite there yet, but I'm working on it.

The greatest haiku poet ever was Basho, who lived almost 400 years ago. He was born into a rich family, but he gave it all up to lead a simple life, wandering around the countryside, writing poetry. I want to live like that, but my father insists that I have to go to college and study medicine. We'll see!

I might change my mind, though, and become a manga-ka instead. That's someone who draws manga. My manga series, which will take fifty issues to complete, will be about a girl who gives up her medical career to lead a simple life, wandering around the countryside, writing poetry. And fighting ninjas.

But right now, before I become a manga-ka or a wandering poet, I'm being a detective. I never dreamed about being a detective before, but it's kind of fun. Before we even started the agency, Bradley says we had already turning foiled a mad scientist who was turning a whole school full of kids into zombies. Who knows what we'll do in the future? Anyway, I like my partners. Raf is really smart, even if he is a year younger than me, and Bradley is not only smart, he's soft and cuddly and cute. (But I never tell him that, because I know it would embarrass him.)

Ice cream: Chocolate or vanilla?
Soy ice cream, any flavor.

Food: Hamburger or fried chicken?
That's gross! I'm a vegetarian, and I won't eat anything that has a face. Soy is awesome!

Best friends:
Raf Hernandez and Bradley

CHICAGOLAND DETECTIVE AGENCY

Name: Bradley

Age: 2

Education: The school of hard knocks

Favorite quote: If you want me, just whistle.

Favorite book: THE KENNEL MURDER CASE, by S. S. Van Dine

Favorite movie: THE KENNEL MURDER CASE. (It was a book first, and then they made it into a movie, a long time ago. The hero, Philo Vance, has a dog and is a detective. On top of being a good detective, he loves his dog, so that's why Philo Vance is my favorite detective.)

Ice cream: Chocolate or vanilla? Gotta be vanilla, in small amounts. Dogs can't eat chocolate--AT ALL. It could kill us!

Food: Hamburger or fried chicken? Hamburger, raw please. Dogs can't eat chicken, either, because the bones could choke us or damage our stomachs. So, pal, if you love your dogs (and I hope you do!), lay off the chocolate and cooked chicken!

Best friends: Raf Hernandez and Megan Yamamura

I never knew my old man, and I can't remember my mom. And if that ain't enough, I spent two years as a captive of a loony dame named Dr. Vorschak. Her fiendish experiments on me turned me into a doggy Einstein. But now I have finally found a family with Raf and Megan. Of course, the world has to think that Raf is the big boss of our detective agency. Only Raf and Megan know that I'm the real brains behind the outfit.

Megan and Raf are swell kids, but they can't be more than sidekicks. Their little tiny noses aren't any good for tracking people by their smell. Dogs can smell fear!

I learned how to be a gumshoe from my heroes, like Philo Vance and Sam Spade. Megan says all those private eyes I watched on Dr. Vorschak's TV aren't real, just made-up characters in books and movies, but to me, they're as real as the slipper I chewed on this morning.

From those old detective movies, I learned that my heroes had a strong sense of justice. They couldn't rest until they solved the crimes and caught the bad guys, and I thought, us dogs are like that. Once we get our teeth into something, we don't wanna let go. A dog's gotta do what a dog's gotta do, so we make good detectives.

We may be small, but we have big hearts!

Trina Robbins made a name for herself in the underground comix movement of the 1960s. She published the first all-woman comic book in the 1970s; published her first history of women cartoonists, *Women and the Comics*, in the 1980s; was an artist for the *Woman Woman* comic book; and created the superhero series *Go Girl!* with artist Anne Timmons. And that's just a start—she has written biographies, other nonfiction, and way too many other books and comics for kids and adults to list, but you can check them out on her website at www.trinarobbins.com. She lives in San Francisco with her partner, comics writer Steve Leialoha.

Tyler Page is an Eisner Award-nominated illustrator and webcomic artist who has self-published four graphic novels, including *Nothing Better*, recipient of a Xeric Foundation Grant. His day job is as director of Print Technology Services at the Minneapolis College of Art and Design, where he oversees the college's print-based facilities. He's been drawing his whole life, and sometime around middle school started making his own comics starring the family cat. He lives with wife Cori Doerrfeld, daughter Charlotte, and two crazy cats in Minneapolis, and his website lives at www.stylishvittles.com.